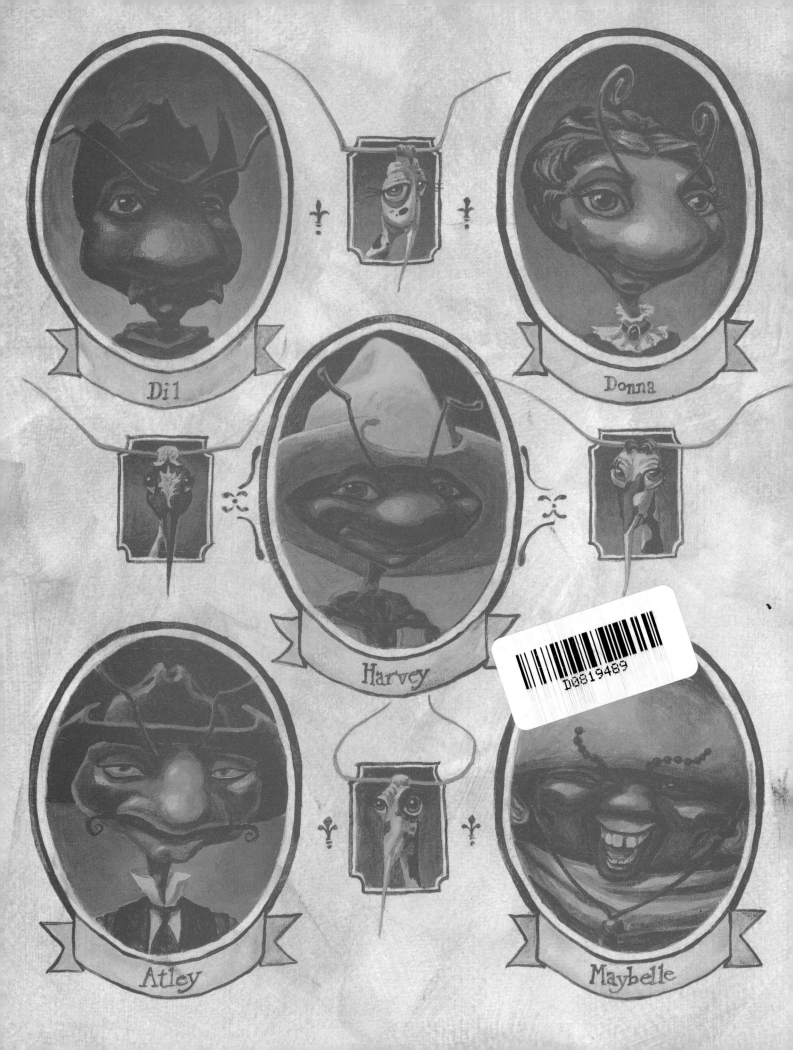

For Emily, my bug-lovin' gal

WAY OUT WEST at the foot of an old cottonwood, there is
a sleepy little town by the name of Ant Hill. Nothing much
ever happens there, and that is just fine with most folks,
especially Deputy Harvey. But this morning was different.
The deputy had just come from the Milking Barn and there
was extra git in his giddyup as he hurried down dusty
Main Street.

Harvey poked his head into the Ant Hill Diner and found the sheriff seated at the counter.

"Sheriff Dil," exclaimed Harvey. "Half the herd has gone missin'!"

"Dawg-gonnit, Harvey. Can't you see I'm eating?" Sheriff Dil shoveled another bite of honeydew cake into his mouth. "How many times I got to tell you? No business before breakfast."

Donna, the waitress, scolded the sheriff. "Dil, didn't you hear Harvey? How can you eat at a time like this? You know every ant in Ant Hill depends on the honeydew those cows produce. No cows, no dew. No dew, no ants. I'd like to know what you plan to do."

The sheriff held out his mug. "Have some more coffee," he grunted.

After a last cup of honeydew coffee, Deputy Harvey convinced Sheriff Dil they should interview the only witness to the disappearing cows. They climbed their way up to the high grazing range and found Clem, the trail boss, keeping a watchful eye over what was left of the herd. "Can't explain it exactly," said Clem. "One minute them cows is sippin' sap as peaceful as you please, the next, they's up and vanished. Thought I saw somethin' moving in the shadows, though. Think it had spots!"

Word of the Polka-dot Bandits spread like a prairie fire up and down Main Street. The mayor called a town hall meeting.

"I'm down to my last barrel of honeydew brew," complained the barkeep.

"The kiddies'll have to do without honeydew sodas and dewdrop candies," said the clerk from the Sweet Shop.

"My shelves will soon be as bare as a willow in winter," warned the owner of the General Store.

Mr. Moody, the foreman down at the Milking Barn, reported the supply of honeydew was getting mighty low. With a gang of ladybugs on the loose, the rest of the cows were most certainly in terrible danger. Yessiree, things were looking mighty grim for the good folks of Ant Hill.

"I believe I have a solution to Ant Hill's problem," said a stranger standing at the back of the room. "Allow me to introduce myself. Atley Diamond of the Diamond A Ranch, at your service. My herd of cows will help make more than enough honeydew to tide you folks over until your fine sheriff and his able deputy can round up those rustlers."

The residents of Ant Hill began to cheer.

All day, Harvey watched folks line up on Main Street to purchase Diamond A Dew. Business was brisk.

"Hmm," thought Harvey. "Atley Diamond rolled into town with a wagon full of honeydew and now he's leaving with a wagon full of money. Odd that none of *his* cows are being stolen. It's high time that somebody put a stop to this thievin' . . . and I know just how to do it too!"

High above Ant Hill, the town's herd dozed on a cottonwood leaf.
Content after a day of sipping sap, they paid no mind to the odd-
looking cow that joined them at sundown.

Suddenly a gang of spotted figures stepped into the moonlight.
One cracked his whip. Another prodded with a stick. A bandit kicked
the new cow and hissed, "Get along, ol' Bossy." Harvey nearly blew his
cover when he felt the boot on his backside.

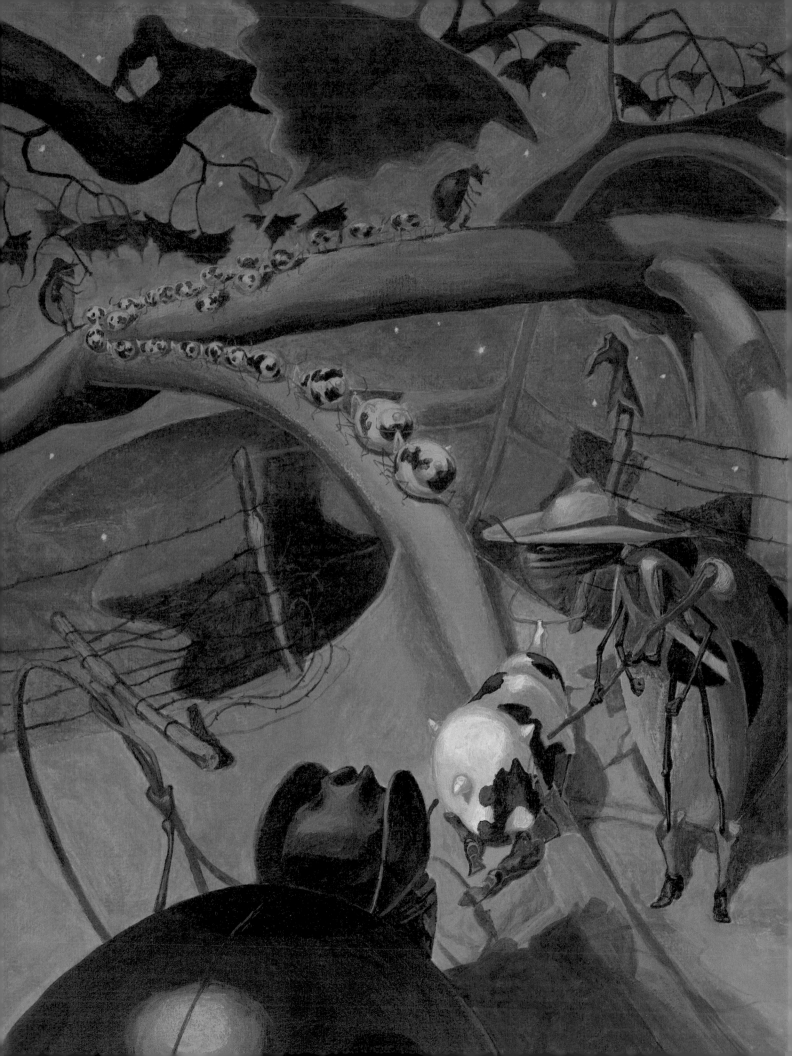

The herd made its way across the leaf, up the stem, and along a branch. On the other side of the tree, Harvey watched the Ant Hill cows enter a shed. When they came out, they had the Diamond A brand—Atley Diamond's brand! "I'll be durned. They're putting Attley's brand on our cows," he thought.

Harvey jumped to his feet, held out his badge, and shouted, "Nobody move. You're all under arrest. And that includes you, Sheriff!" Harvey pointed to the outlaw who had booted his behind.

Sheriff Dil lowered the bandanna covering his face and shrugged off the fake polka-dot shell. "Deputy Harvey, I do declare. Disguised as a skinny ol' cow. Very clever for a fellow with a ten-gallon hat and a two-gallon brain—very clever, indeed! But we don't much want to go to jail and you can't put us there, seeing how you're out-manned."

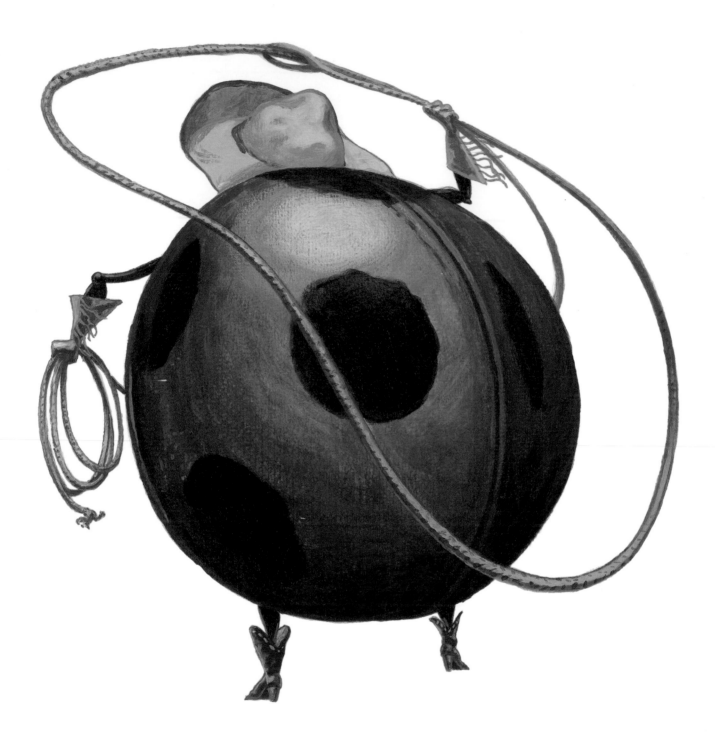

The ants jumped at the sound of the husky voice. Standing before them was a very angry ladybug. "Grab 'em, girls," she bellowed. There was a buzz and a flash of moonlight on gleaming shells. When the dust settled, Sheriff Dil and his gang were wrapped in rope, surrounded by a pack of ladybugs—*real* ladybugs.

The leader stepped up to Harvey and tipped her hat. "Howdy, Deputy. My name's Maybelle, queen beetle in this little band of bugs. We heard how some bandits pretendin' to be ladybugs was stealin' a whole herd of ant cows. Couldn't stand by and let a pack of no-good criminals tarnish our reputation."

"I sure do thank you, ma'am," said Harvey. "I'm awful sorry for suspecting y'all were behind this bad business."

"Aw shucks, Deputy. It all turned out in the end. Just you set things straight with the townsfolk, now. Wouldn't want 'em thinking ill of ol' Maybelle and her gals. See ya down the trail somewheres."

Next morning, Harvey was sipping coffee at the Ant Hill Diner. Donna carried over a stack of honeydew cakes. "On the house, Deputy— I mean Sheriff. It's the least I can do. After all, you rescued the herd and saved the town. I guess the sheriff, Atley, and their bunch are behind bars where they belong."

"Well, not exactly…" said Harvey, savoring a mouthful of honeydew cake.

"I put them to work down at the Milking Barn. You know all those cows produce an awful lot of *doo*!"

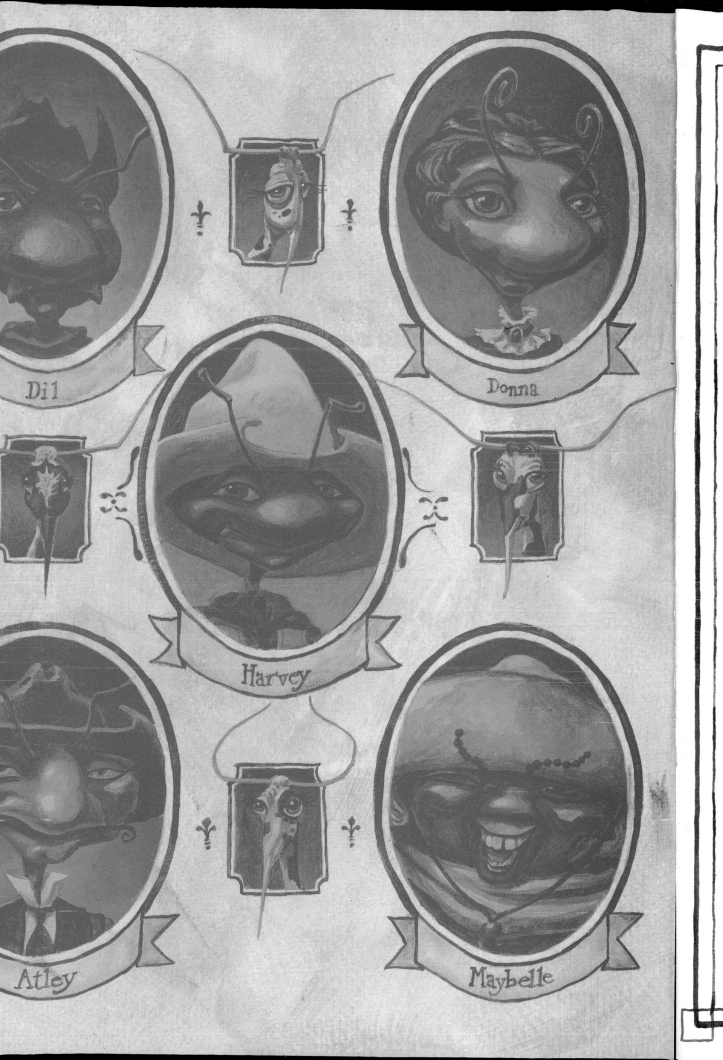

Author's Note

Did you know that "ant cow" is a nickname for a tiny insect called an aphid? We people like to drink cow's milk, and it so happens that aphids make a sweet juice, called honeydew, that ants like to eat. Aphids live on plants and spend most of their day sucking sap from a leaf or stem. The sap is turned into honeydew, which ants find delicious. Sometimes they will even round up a herd of aphids just so they can have honeydew anytime they please. When an ant is hungry for fresh dew, it taps the aphid with its antennae and the aphid squirts out a drop of honeydew. Bug scientists call this "milking."

Ants help aphids too. They are much bigger and protect the little aphids from being eaten by ladybugs, lacewings, and other hungry insects. And the ants will move aphid herds from plant to plant or even drive them to underground tunnels in bad weather!

There are many kinds of aphids all around the world. Check out your own backyard or the neighborhood park. If you see a plant with ants walking along its stems, look closely at the underside of the leaves. You may find a herd of tiny ant cows sippin' sap and makin' dew!

Dial Books for Young Readers
A division of Penguin Young Readers Group
Published by The Penguin Group
Penguin Group (USA) Inc., 375 Hudson Street, New York, NY 10014, U.S.A.

Penguin Group (Canada), 10 Alcorn Avenue, Toronto, Ontario, Canada M4V 3B2
(a division of Pearson Penguin Canada Inc.) Penguin Books Ltd, 80 Strand, London WC2R 0RL, England
Penguin Ireland, 25 St. Stephen's Green, Dublin 2, Ireland (a division of Penguin Books Ltd)
Penguin Group (Australia), 250 Camberwell Road, Camberwell, Victoria 3124, Australia
(a division of Pearson Australia Group Pty Ltd)
Penguin Books India Pvt Ltd, 11 Community Centre, Panchsheel Park, New Delhi - 110 017, India
Penguin Group (NZ), Cnr Airborne and Rosedale Roads, Albany, Auckland 1310, New Zealand
(a division of Pearson New Zealand Ltd)
Penguin Books (South Africa) (Pty) Ltd, 24 Sturdee Avenue, Rosebank, Johannesburg 2196,
South Africa Penguin Books Ltd, Registered Offices: 80 Strand, London WC2R 0RL, England

Typography by Nancy R. Leo-Kelly
Text set in New Century Schoolbook
Manufactured in China on acid-free paper
1 3 5 7 9 10 8 6 4 2

Library of Congress Cataloging-in-Publication Data
Sneed, Brad.
Deputy Harvey and the ant cow caper / Brad Sneed.
p.   cm.
Summary: The sheriff of Ant Hill seems none too worried when he's informed
that someone—perhaps a gang of ladybugs—has been rustling their ant cows,
but Deputy Harvey is determined to put a stop to the thievery.
ISBN 0-8037-3023-3
[1. Sheriffs—Fiction. 2. Ants—Fiction. 3. Insects—Fiction.
4. Robbers and outlaws—Fiction. 5. West (U.S.)—Fiction.] I. Title.
PZ7.S6713De 2005   [E]—dc22   2004008102

The artwork for this book was created with acrylic on paper.

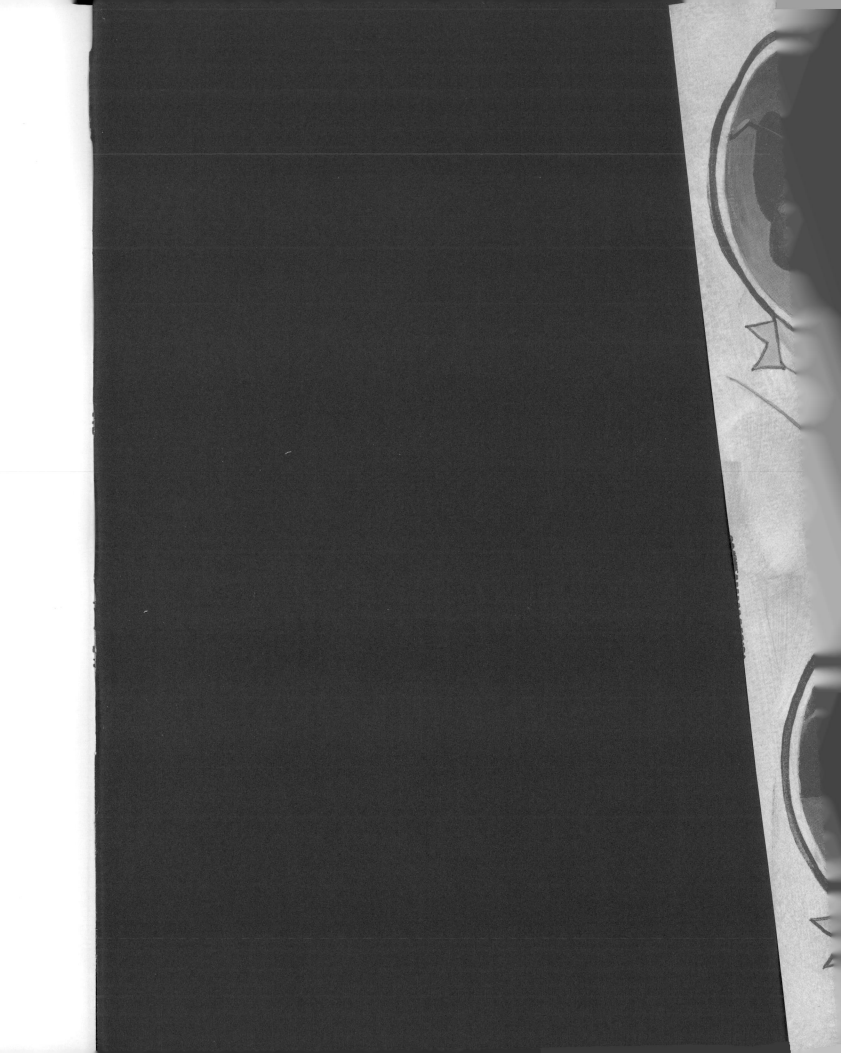

Author's Note

Did you know that "ant cow" is a nickname for a tiny insect called an aphid? We people like to drink cow's milk, and it so happens that aphids make a sweet juice, called honeydew, that ants like to eat. Aphids live on plants and spend most of their day sucking sap from a leaf or stem. The sap is turned into honeydew, which ants find delicious. Sometimes they will even round up a herd of aphids just so they can have honeydew anytime they please. When an ant is hungry for fresh dew, it taps the aphid with its antennae and the aphid squirts out a drop of honeydew. Bug scientists call this "milking."

Ants help aphids too. They are much bigger and protect the little aphids from being eaten by ladybugs, lacewings, and other hungry insects. And the ants will move aphid herds from plant to plant or even drive them to underground tunnels in bad weather!

There are many kinds of aphids all around the world. Check out your own backyard or the neighborhood park. If you see a plant with ants walking along its stems, look closely at the underside of the leaves. You may find a herd of tiny ant cows sippin' sap and makin' dew!

Dial Books for Young Readers
A division of Penguin Young Readers Group
Published by The Penguin Group
Penguin Group (USA) Inc., 375 Hudson Street, New York, NY 10014, U.S.A.

Penguin Group (Canada), 10 Alcorn Avenue, Toronto, Ontario, Canada M4V 3B2
(a division of Pearson Penguin Canada Inc.) Penguin Books Ltd, 80 Strand, London WC2R 0RL, England
Penguin Ireland, 25 St. Stephen's Green, Dublin 2, Ireland (a division of Penguin Books Ltd)
Penguin Group (Australia), 250 Camberwell Road, Camberwell, Victoria 3124, Australia
(a division of Pearson Australia Group Pty Ltd)
Penguin Books India Pvt Ltd, 11 Community Centre, Panchsheel Park, New Delhi - 110 017, India
Penguin Group (NZ), Cnr Airborne and Rosedale Roads, Albany, Auckland 1310, New Zealand
(a division of Pearson New Zealand Ltd)
Penguin Books (South Africa) (Pty) Ltd, 24 Sturdee Avenue, Rosebank, Johannesburg 2196,
South Africa Penguin Books Ltd, Registered Offices: 80 Strand, London WC2R 0RL, England

Typography by Nancy R. Leo-Kelly
Text set in New Century Schoolbook
Manufactured in China on acid-free paper
1 3 5 7 9 10 8 6 4 2

Library of Congress Cataloging-in-Publication Data
Sneed, Brad.
Deputy Harvey and the ant cow caper / Brad Sneed.
p.   cm.
Summary: The sheriff of Ant Hill seems none too worried when he's informed
that someone—perhaps a gang of ladybugs—has been rustling their ant cows,
but Deputy Harvey is determined to put a stop to the thievery.
ISBN 0-8037-3023-3
[1. Sheriffs—Fiction. 2. Ants—Fiction. 3. Insects—Fiction.
4. Robbers and outlaws—Fiction. 5. West (U.S.)—Fiction.] I. Title.
PZ7.S6713De 2005   [E]—dc22   2004008102

The artwork for this book was created with acrylic on paper.

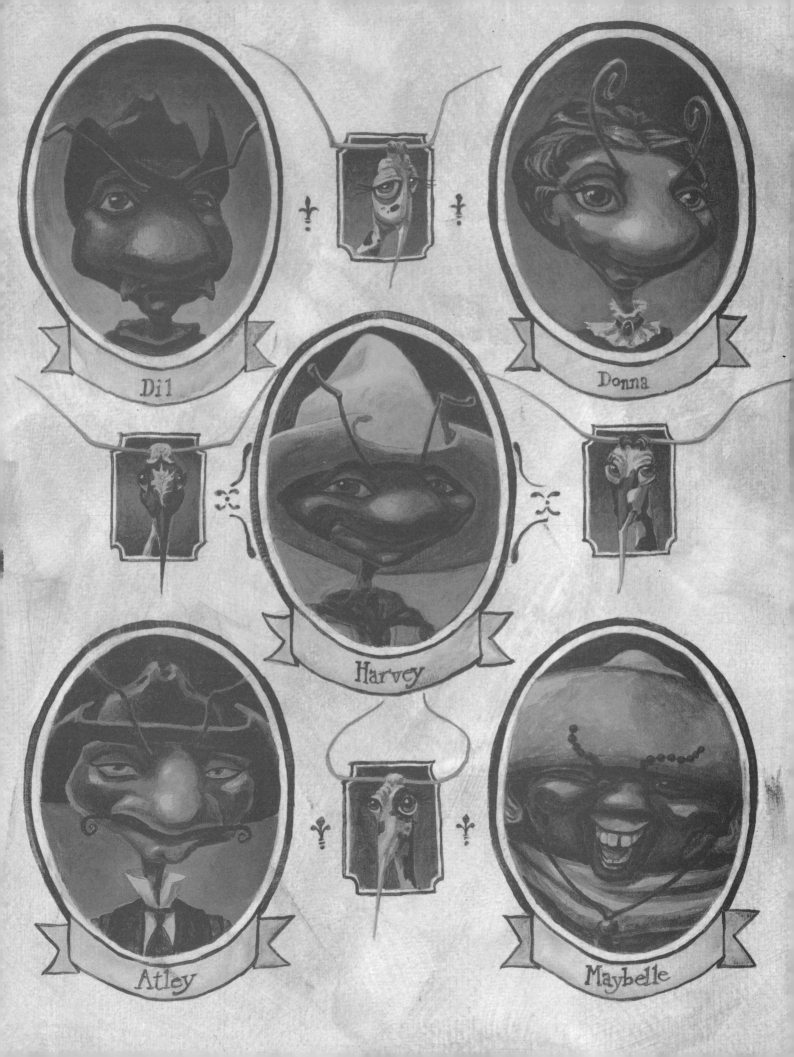